The Kindness Weapon

by Bruce Wannamaker
illustrated by
Susan Lexa

Published by The Dandelion House
A Division of The Child's World

for distribution by BOOKS a division of SP Publications, Inc.
WHEATON, ILLINOIS 60187

Offices also in
Whitby, Ontario, Canada
Amersham-on-the-Hill, Bucks, England

Published by The Dandelion House, A Division of The Child's World, Inc.
© 1984 SP Publications, Inc. All rights reserved. Printed in U.S.A.

A Book for Early Readers.

Library of Congress Cataloging in Publication Data

_____.

The kindness weapon.

Summary: A boy's kindness helps a friend recover
after an accident which leaves him unable to walk.
[1. Kindness—Fiction.   2. Christian life—
Fiction]   I. Lexa, Susan, ill.   II. Title.
PZ7.M739Ki   1984   [E]   84-7038
ISBN 0-89693-219-2

1 2 3 4 5 6 7 8 9 10 11 12 R 90 89 88 87 86 85 84

The
Kindness
Weapon

Joe and Ricky were best friends. They lived right next door to each other. They rode bikes together, ate lunch together at school, were in the same Sunday School class, and played on the same soccer team.

They also shared a favorite place. It was in the branches of a big oak tree that grew between their back yards.

"You know what?" said Ricky one day. "This tree would make a good hideout. Let's build a tree house and have a secret club."

"Good idea," said Joe. "Our dads will help. I know they will."

"Let's build it right after school is out this summer," said Ricky.

"Sounds good," said Joe.

But as soon as school was out, Ricky went with his mom and dad to Arizona. They went to spend the summer with Ricky's grandmother.

Joe went to camp. He had fun swimming and hiking, but he missed Ricky.

He wrote Ricky a letter, but Ricky never answered it.

Joe was disappointed. He wondered why Ricky didn't write.

Then came the terrible news.

Ricky's mother wrote that Ricky had been hurt in an automobile accident. Joe's parents sent a card. Joe put a note inside. At Sunday School everyone prayed for Ricky.

Joe didn't realize how badly Ricky had been hurt until Ricky came home in August. His dad rolled him out of the van in a wheelchair.

Joe felt awful. He wanted to say, "Ricky, I'm sorry—will you ever walk again? How did the accident happen?" But all that came out was, "Hi, Ricky."

After Ricky's dad rolled Ricky into the house, he came back outside.

"Will Ricky walk again?" Joe asked.

"I don't know," said Ricky's father. "The doctors aren't sure either."

Joe ran home. Mom was in the kitchen. "Mom, Ricky can't walk—maybe never . . . ever. Why did God let this happen?" he asked.

Mom stopped cooking and sat beside Joe at the kitchen table. She said, "Sometimes things happen that we just don't understand. But we must not blame God."

"But Ricky may never get well," said Joe. "What if Ricky can never walk again?"

"Joe, let's not give up so quickly. No one is sure that Ricky will never walk. When someone we love is sick or hurt, we should fight to help him win his battle. And we should fight with very special kinds of weapons.

"We should fight with weapons of courage and hope and prayer."

"And—I remember—the kindness weapon!" said Joe. "That's what you used when I was sick."

"That's right," said his mom.

"So now that Ricky is hurt, I'll use the kindness weapon to make him feel better," said Joe.

That very afternoon Joe took his favorite
game next door.

At first Ricky didn't want to play. He didn't want to do anything.

But Joe showed him his new football game for two players. Ricky liked it.

"Hey, maybe I can't kick a football with my feet, but I can play with my fingers!" said Ricky.

Joe knew his kindness weapon was working!

On Sunday, Joe told the Sunday School class
about how he was trying to help Ricky.

"You know," said his teacher, "you are
being a Good Samaritan. Remember how the
man from Samaria helped a man who had
been robbed and beaten? We call him the
Good Samaritan. We want to be like him."

"I helped my sister when she had a broken arm," said Beth.

"I found a little hurt kitten once," said Heather, "and we took it to the animal shelter."

"When my uncle's car skidded off the road, a truck driver stopped to help. He called the highway patrol on his CB radio," said Tommy.

"We all could do something for Ricky," said Joe.

"I know," said Beth. "Let's make him a get-well ball. Let's write little messages and

put them in a ball of yarn. Then, when Ricky un-winds the yarn, they will fall out one at a time."

They all wrote messages to Ricky. When the ball was finished, Joe took it to Ricky.

Ricky liked the get-well ball. He smiled as he read the messages.

19

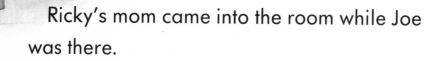

Ricky's mom came into the room while Joe was there.

"The doctor says Ricky must begin to exercise his legs," said Ricky's mom.

"But it hurts," said Ricky. "I can't."

"Come on, Ricky," said Joe. "Start by wiggling your toes! You have to fight."

"That's what Ricky needs—encouragement," said his mom.

"Come on, Ricky. All your friends are rooting for you."

Ricky wiggled his toes, and again Joe knew
his kindness weapon was working.

As the months passed, Joe did many kind things for Ricky. He brought assignments home from school. He studied with Ricky each night.

A tutor came to help Ricky each week, and a therapist came each weekend. The therapist moved Ricky's legs and tried to get him to use them.

But as fall turned into winter, Ricky showed very little improvement.

On a snowy day in March, Joe built a snow-
man in Ricky's front yard. Ricky waved from
the window, but he looked so pale and crum-
pled in his wheelchair that Joe cried on the
inside.

But he waved back. And he didn't act sad
when he went inside to share some cookies and
a cup of hot chocolate with Ricky.

Week after week, Joe did all that he could for his friend. Still, Ricky remained in the wheelchair.

One warm spring day, when Joe's dad was planting a garden, Joe talked with him. "Why doesn't God make Ricky well?" he asked.

"I don't know, Son. But I do know we should keep praying. Maybe Ricky needs to fight harder himself. The doctor has said he can walk if he wants to. Maybe he needs something to really make him want to use those legs again."

Joe thought about what his dad said. Then he remembered something Ricky really wanted—the tree house! Surely Ricky would want to use his legs to climb into it!

Joe told his dad about the tree house.
His dad said he would help build it.

"If you can put up ten dollars, I'll buy the rest
of the lumber," he said.

Joe took all the money out of his bank. He had only three dollars. So he did extra jobs. He helped his mom wash the windows one Saturday morning. He earned a dollar.

Then he helped Mr. Allen unload a pile of
wood from his pick-up truck. He earned
two dollars.

He took care of the Williamsons' dog while
they were away on a trip, and earned four
dollars. Now he had the money for the lumber.

But when Joe's dad called Ricky's dad about building the tree house, the news he heard about Ricky wasn't good. Ricky was being taken to the hospital in Morgantown for therapy. He would be away a month.

"I don't know," said Joe. "Maybe we shouldn't build the tree house now. Ricky isn't even here!"

"Maybe this is the best time to build it," said his mom. "Make it a surprise! Make a big bang with your kindness weapon!"

"Yeah!" said Joe. "A surprise for Ricky. That's it."

During the next few weekends, Joe and his
dad built the tree house. It wasn't very high,
but it would be a good hideout.

When Ricky came home, his dad and Joe rolled him outside to see the tree house. His mom came outside too.

"Wow!" said Ricky. "It's all done! How'd you do it without me?"

"Oh, we just did part of the job," said Joe.

"What do you mean?"

"We left some boards for you to nail to-gether when you climb up there!" said Joe.

Ricky looked down. "But I can't climb," he said. "I can't even walk."

"Dr. Winn says your legs are strong enough," said Ricky's dad. "He said it's up to you to start moving them again."

"I do want to go up in the tree house," said Ricky.

"I'll hold you up," said his dad, "while you try to walk."

"Come on," said Joe. "You can lean on me."

Very slowly, Ricky stood up. His dad held one arm. Joe held the other. Ricky moved his foot forward!

"He did it!" shouted Joe.

"He really did!" said Ricky's mom.

"I can walk!" said Ricky.

It was some time before Ricky could climb into the tree house. But he did that, too, one warm July afternoon.

"Joe should get a prize for helping Ricky through this," said Ricky's mom.

Joe's mom smiled. "You know," she said, "Joe already has a prize. It's his secret gift. He calls it his kindness weapon. I hope he keeps it, always."